HIS DIRTY SECRET 11

SIDE CHICK CONFESSIONS BOOK 11

MIA BLACK

CHAPTER 1

Jayla

The birds whistling outside let me know that it was morning. My room was still completely dark because as always, I had the blinds closed tight. It was hard to tell what time of day it was, but hearing the birds chirping was a clue that the sun was probably up. The sound of their chatter filled my room and a part of me wanted to get up, open the blinds, and just look out the window. I wanted to see them and watch the sun bring in a new day, but I couldn't move. I just stared out in the darkness. It felt like something was keeping me on my bed, but I couldn't put my finger on it.

There were so many things running around in my head and I didn't know which one to blame it on first.

Why couldn't my life be normal? Why couldn't my life look like something from those sappy TV shows or the movies? My life had so much drama; especially my love life. Why couldn't my love life just be about two people meeting, finding out they are attracted to each other, falling madly in love, and just living happily ever after? Why couldn't I have that? Why does my love life have to be something out of an HBO movie? It was always dark, gritty, and full of drama. It was never simple. Every one of these relationships were so dramatic and I just wanted one to be simple. Was that too much to ask for?

Shane was supposed to be simple. Shane was supposed to be the opposite of what happened back in Atlanta with Darius. It was supposed to be so easy and that's how it started out. It was just so good in the beginning. Even though I fought to stay away from him, Shane drew me in. His personality, his smile, his body, just everything about that man was magnetic. From the moment I met him, I wanted him. I was trying my hardest not to, but I couldn't help it. The feeling started slow and with one touch it took over my body, my mind, and my heart. I kept trying to deny it, but I was falling for him. It didn't take long from there for drama to pop its ugly head.

Tossing and turning in bed, I tried to escape the thoughts that were racing in my mind. I was being flooded with memories. Every memory of us together came in. The first time he kissed me kept playing over and over in my head. His lips touched mine and the fire in me went crazy. Just one touch and I knew that I was going to be hooked. I didn't want to stop kissing him and even though that thought scared me, it still felt good. Being with Shanc was like an addiction. I was so gone over him and that's how bullshit snuck its way in.

I never thought that I could become a victim. I knew that drama could get me into some shit, but lately it had been getting worse. I really thought holding Darius' dead body was the worst thing that could happen. I thought that shit couldn't get any worse than that, but I was wrong. Miles away from

Atlanta, Damaiah, Shane's ex and baby mama, brought me to a place that I couldn't imagine. As soon as she found out that I was with Shane, she hated me with a passion. She popped up at my job, threatened me, and even fought me. After all that, I should have went running away and never looked back. Fuck love, I should have been thinking about my brother and my sister, and of course my own life. I should have put them first before I did that relationship, but I loved Shane so I stayed. I thought he had it under control and he said he did, but Damiah had us looking stupid. She pretended that everything was fine and then she tried to kill me.

Now that I think about it, I cheated death twice, and both times it was because I fell in love. I fell in love with Darius. He had a wife, but it didn't matter because I loved him. The next thing I knew I was holding his dead body right outside my place. Now it was me almost dying and again it was over a new dude. What am I doing with my life?

There was a soft knock at the door. It creaked slowly and light poured in my room.

"Sis." Keon's voice was soft but very

tired. With him saying that one word, I could hear his pain behind it. He's really been there for me throughout everything. I honestly don't know what I would have done without him or his girlfriend Crystal. Slowly, I turned around and squinted at him. He gave me a small smile, but I knew he was only doing it to make me feel better. His eyes were restless and he was trying his best not to show it.

"How you doing?" He didn't step into my bedroom but leaned on the door frame. He reached to turn on my light but I told him not to. "Come on Jayla." He sighed. "You should get out of bed."

"I'm okay. I'm fine," I mumbled, holding on to the covers even more. My body started to stiffen up.

"Come on, let's have some lunch."

"Lunch? It's still early in the morning."

"Jayla, it's after 12 p.m.," he informed me. I turned and looked at the alarm clock that was right on my nightstand. It read 12:53. Where did all the time ago?

"Oh," I said, but still I felt my body come more at ease with my bed. I felt safe there.

"We'll just go get some chicken, some juice, rice, and everything else you like."

"I'm not hungry," I whispered, lying because I didn't want to get out of bed.

"Please."

The tone in his voice moved me. Even though I was looking at this grown ass man asking me to leave my bedroom, when he spoke all I saw was the young boy that I use to look after back in Chicago. I looked at him and just saw my baby brother. His eyes were trying to do what his arms couldn't; it was trying to pull me out of bed. My body got stiff again and I sunk deeper into bed.

"Keon…" I started thinking of what I could tell my little brother that would make him understand, but honestly I didn't really understand what was going on right now.

"Jayla, you've been in bed all weekend."

"I'm just tired."

"Look." He sat on the edge of the bed. "I know that you've been through a lot Sis, and I can't imagine what you're still going through now after the fact, but you can't stay in your room like this. You can't live your life like this."

"But…" I felt the truth trying to come out of me. "It hurts," I confessed.

Once I heard myself say the words, a sense of relief washed over me. I finally put words to the what I was feeling. I thought it was just me feeling afraid but not only that…I was hurting.

"I know it hurts and I wish I could take that pain away from you, but in some way, I don't have to worry about you. Do you know why?"

"Why?"

"Because you're a survivor sis. Look at all the shit you've been through."

"Yeah and it broke me." I started to cry.

"You're not broken Jayla, you're just down for a little bit, but this will not end you. You can make it." He grinned. "Fuck that, you *have* made it and you just need to get out of this room and this house. You've been here all weekend and you barely ate."

"I'm not hung—"

"You can stop that lying." He cut me off. "You've lost some weight Jayla."

He was concerned and I understood. I was practically living in my bedroom at this point.

I don't really go to work. Me and my bed are beyond best friends at this point. I finally started moving and made my way to the bathroom. On the way there, I passed by the mirror and stopped short. I didn't even recognize myself. My eyes had bags underneath them, my face looked so tired, my hair was a mess, and my clothes were so baggy. I walked closer and touched the mirror. I couldn't believe what I've come to. Keon looked at me through the mirror. He didn't have to say anything, but it wasn't necessary.

"Let me go take a shower."

The hot water hit my body and it woke every part of my body up. The steam filled up the rooms and out of nowhere, I started crying a little bit. Just thinking about everything was sad enough, but then I thought about how much of it affected Keon. He was about to finish school but he had to deal with the drama from his big sister's life. I'm so grateful for him and his girlfriend Crystal. Crystal wasn't even family but she felt like another little sister to me. It was nice to turn to her because I didn't want to bother my other little sister who was away at college. She always called and emailed me telling me how much fun she was having and how much she was learning. I didn't tell her anything and didn't mind when she told me that she was trying to go to school throughout the whole year. I didn't want her to see me like this.

After my shower, I put on some lotion and got dressed. Grabbing some makeup, I tried to make myself look decent. Back in Atlanta, Charmaine use to always say that you had to look good before you felt good. Maybe if I actually put some effort today, I might start feeling a little better. I grabbed the brush and started to brush my hair into a neat top bun. It started to hurt, making me realize how much I really let myself go. When that was done, I put on some light makeup so that my bags could disappear. I was starting to look decent enough so I threw on a cute sweatsuit outfit and made my way out.

Keon and I went to a soul food restaurant. The whole drive there Keon turned on the radio and kept it on a station that played old school hip hop. We were rapping along to Notorious BIG, Tupac, Ice Cube, Snoop, NWA, and just all the old school artist of the

90s. It was good to have fun and for just a moment, I forgot about everything. We were laughing and smiling trying to remember all the words to the songs.

"Damn, I haven't seen you smile in so long." Keon laughed and he was smiling too. "It's nice to see, Sis."

We sat in the soul food restaurant in a booth. I kept telling Keon earlier that I wasn't hungry, but when I sat there and smelled all the food, my mouth started watering. I looked over the menu and before I knew it, I ordered steak and potatoes, fried chicken, and some mac and cheese. Minutes later my fork was going like crazy. Keon kept looking at me with a look on his face.

"What?" I asked after he'd been staring for a long time.

"I thought you said you weren't hungry," he teased. I laughed looking down at my empty plate and we both started laughing.

It was nice to be out my room. My brother looked so happy. He must have really missed his big sister. I felt the guilt come over me, but I pushed it away and focused on the moment.

"So, what's been going on with you?" I

asked. "I feel like we talk about me all the time." I sighed. "How's things going on with school?"

"I'm almost done and I might have some potential jobs lined up."

"That's good." I smiled. "I'm so proud of you."

"I just wanted to let you know I'm grateful for all that you've done for me."

"Keon…" I didn't want to hear anything gushy right now. I felt like anything could make me cry.

"Nah, let me get this out." He put his fork down and looked at me. "I remember how I was back in the day. I was out there being a knucklehead and wasn't listening to nobody. I put you through a lot of shit, but you never really gave up on me. I know that me and you butt heads, but you always had faith in me. I could feel that you wanted me to do more, so it made it easier for me to turn my life around. It was like I had to do this for myself and for you. Now that I see where I am, I know that's because of you. You've done a lot for me."

I tried not to cry but hearing Keon say

these words to me made me start sobbing quietly.

"Damn, I didn't mean for you to be out here crying." He had a slight smirk on his face. "You so emotional. You suppose to give me thug tears."

"What?" I started laughing. "What the fuck are thug tears?"

"It's when you let one tear slide down your face." He smiled.

"Boy, you stupid. But thank you for saying that." I wiped the tears from my face. "Got my makeup coming off and shit." I chuckled. "Tell me something else. Tell me about Crystal."

"I'm surprised that wasn't the first thing you asked, with your nosey ass."

I felt all happy because I knew what he was talking about. Before the whole bullshit with Damiah went down, Keon surprised me by telling me that he was going to propose to his girlfriend.

"Well, I didn't want to ask you and you felt like you were being pressured or something."

"How am I going to be pressured when I am the one that brought it up?" He shook his head. "But for your information, I am still planning on proposing to her."

"Have you thought about how?"

"Nah, but I know I want it to be soon."

"Aw damn." I felt a tear coming out. "You're so happy."

"You can be happy too."

I nodded when he said that and hoped one day, he would be right.

CHAPTER 2

Jayla

Monday rolled in the next day and I decided that it was time for me to concentrate on work. Usually I would go for three or four days out of the week, but enough was enough. Keon was right; I could no longer live my life in my bedroom. Pulling up to the parking lot of my job, I took a deep breath. When I would get to the parking lot, flashbacks of Damiah would pop in. She came up to my job and we got into a screaming match in this parking lot. I couldn't wait for those memories to fade away, but that was not happening no time soon.

"Hey girl." Samara was at the front desk talking to the receptionist. Of course every time I saw her, I thought about her brother Shane. It was one of the reasons why I couldn't hang out with her like I use to.

"Good morning." I greeted her with a small hug. "How is everything here? Is it crazy?"

"No, it's real slow today. Everyone has been real chill, it's going to be a nice day." She and I started walking the halls.

"How are you?" I asked her.

"I'm good."

"Is that all?" I squinted at her. I may not hang around her all the time, but I could still tell when there was something going on with her.

"What do you mean?" She was trying to play shy and when she saw my face, she knew it wasn't working. "Okay, I'll tell you."

We were by the lockers in the breakroom. I began putting my things away, still waiting on this tea she was about to spill. Finally, she began talking.

"Well, I have this date," she said slowly with a small smile.

"A date?" I was surprised. I knew she had some situation with her baby father, so I didn't think she would be really dating, but I guess even she could move on. What was holding me up?

"Yes, a date." Her eyes got real wide.

"Wow, I thought you were going to *think* about dating. I didn't know you were actually going to start."

"I can't be stuck on my babyfather like that." She shook her head. "I have a life to live, you know."

"I get it. So, tell me more about him."

"He's just a dude that I met at the library."

"Library?" I gave her the side eye. "What were you doing there?" I teased.

"Girl." She rolled her eyes. "I needed to make a copy of this form and the supervisor here was giving me a problem. You would think that she bought the ink and paper herself for the copy machines. Jayla, I even told her that I would give her a quarter to make a copy here, but she wouldn't take it."

I started busting out laughing. Samara's facials expressions had me cracking up. I could picture her and the supervisor going back and forth over the copy machine. Our supervisor was kind of strict and did act like she built the nursing home with her own two hands. If Samara wanted to make a copy, our supervisor was going to give her a hard time about it.

"So, you went to the library…" I wanted to know more.

"Yeah, so I was at the library trying to work the copy machine when he came up to me."

"Ooooh, what's his name? How does he look like?"

"He's tall, caramel skin, has a lowcut hair style, beautiful smile, and has a little body on him."

"He sounds cute."

"He is, but I don't know, girl." She sighed.

"What do you mean?"

"I mean that there is just something that I can't put my finger on. You know that gut feeling?"

"I do."

I was smiling, but I felt uncomfortable. It just reminded me of everything that I went through with Shane. I hated that I could hear some words and immediately feel depressed over Shane again. I didn't want to live like this anymore. I was ready for it all to be over.

"Anyway," she continued. "He helped me out because with that machine you have to turn on the scanner first and then switch it over to copy. We started talking and we agreed to go out on a date."

"That's good."

"Now, I'm trying to figure out what I'm going to wear. I'm not trying to wear anything too revealing but when you're built thick like me…" She started laughing and I joined in. Samara was thick and she always said that no matter what she wore, it looked like a club outfit. Everything hugged her body a little too much.

"You'll find something." I went over to the soda machine and ordered a seltzer water. "How about during our lunch break we go online and look at some outfits?"

"Yes!" She jumped for joy. "See, this is why I fucks with you. You always have good ideas Jayla."

After work was finished, Samara went straight to the store to pick out the outfit we chose. We both agreed on a nice jumpsuit with some cute sandals. She gave me a hug and kiss before we left each other. It was nice to hang out with her again or even just hanging out with people period.

Before I got to my car, my cell went off. I looked at the screen and smiled when I saw that it was my friend Kim. Kim lived back in Atlanta with Charmaine. She was always the cool and level headed one between me and Charmaine. She had a killer fashion sense and she still sends me outfits that she thinks would look good on me.

"Heyyyyyyyyy." I smiled just thinking of Kim on the other line.

"Heyyyyy," she repeated back to me. Hearing her voice made me feel at home. "How are things chica?"

"Things are getting better. I actually came from work."

"Was it a good day?"

"It was really good. I really like this place. It's so much better than the place where you, me, and Charmaine worked."

"Oooh, I'm so jealous," she teased. "But for real, how are you doing? Are you okay?

With all that went down Jayla, are you doing alright?"

It didn't take long for me to know what she was talking about. I closed my eyes as I took a deep breath. I didn't want my nerves to get the best of me and for me to get depressed all over again. I really did have a good day and I wouldn't let the memories of the bullshit that went down with Damiah and Shane get me down. So before I spoke about it, I just told myself that everything was fine. I reminded myself that Damiah and Trell were both in prison and not going anywhere.

"You know," I started slowly making sure that I didn't get scared or anything. "I was in such a shitty place for the past few weeks. I barely left my bedroom and I didn't really go to work. I was really depressed, and I think nervous." I paused leaning against my car door. "No, not nervous, anxious. I was suffering from anxiety because I didn't even want to leave my room because I was sure that something was going to happen to me. But Keon pulled me out of the house and when I saw that everything was fine, I could believe it more."

"That's good."

"Yeah and plus I think I needed to be sad in bed for a while. I needed to go through that phase so that I would hopefully get over it."

"That sounds really good Jayla."

"But there's one thing though that still bothers me. It still just sits in my gut and I don't know what to do with it.

"What?"

"I still have feelings for Shane."

It was the first time that I'd ever told anyone that. It was good to finally get it out, but at the same time I felt stupid. How could I still like someone after all that has happened to me? Everything that went down with Damiah was Shane's fault, but somehow, I still had feelings for him. I wish that I could just turn it off and go about my business, but that's not how it works.

"I still think about him, I still have feelings about him, and I still want him." I went on to tell her.

"That makes sense though." She was always so understanding. "You had real feelings for him and you fell in love with him.

Those aren't things that are just going to go away because you want them to."

"What should I do?"

"I think maybe you should try dating other guys."

"Dating other guys?" I shook my head. "Dating is the last thing on my mind. I'm not trying to get into another relationship."

"I didn't say all that now." She chuckled. "But sometimes it helps to get out there and see that there are other guys out there. I'm not saying get into a relationship or even to have sex; I just think you need to see that there are other guys out there besides Shane. Just have a little bit of fun."

"Just fun?"

"Yes, just fun. Besides, you need to get back to you. You need to get back to doing the things you liked doing before you got with Shane. You used to go to the gym and all that stuff. Maybe it's time you get back to doing that and trying to get your mind right. You're ready now."

I nodded my head to all that Kim was saying. She was 100% right. I needed to get back to me. The time for feeling depressed is over.

When I got home, I immediately went to my closet. I picked out some gym outfits and some sneakers. I got my water bottle and everything ready for the morning. It was time to bring back the old and happy Jayla.

CHAPTER 3

Jayla

The next morning, I opted out of going to the gym because I remembered that Shane had a lot of gyms in Houston. Before I started going to the gym, I had to make sure it wasn't his first. Instead, I did a light workout at the house. I started with some pushups, but my arms felt weak. It had been so long since I worked out, that everything started to hurt. I pushed past the pain though and continued. After completing many sets of crunches, sit ups, and planks, I felt good. The workout was just what I needed, but I knew I needed more.

The past few weeks in bed taught me one

thing, I was depressed. This was more than just a sadness though and I knew that even though I felt better now, I needed some professional help. I couldn't get well on my own. Grabbing my laptop, I sat down on my bed and began searching for someone to help me mentally. My mental health is really important and getting help with it was high on my list of priorities. After searching for a long time, I finally found a counselor that seemed a great fit. He had very nice reviews online and he was even the same religious background as me. Even though I haven't stepped in a church in years, knowing that we had that same background made me feel better. Luckily, I could book an appointment online. Since today was my day off, I thought that I should get it over with today before I punked out.

Driving up to the facility made me nervous. I gripped the steering wheel as I parked my car. My appointment was in 20 minutes. I watched people go in and out of the building. I wonder what they were in for. Were their stories as bad as mine? Did they go through something worse than me? As I watched more people go in and out of the building, it all clicked. They were all there to get help, which was exactly what I wanted and needed. So I took a deep breath, said a small prayer, and get out of the car. I waited in the lobby still nervous, but determined to see the doctor.

It was finally time for my appointment and my heart was racing. While I was walking to the counselor office, I noticed a picture of him on the wall. He was black, in his mid 50s, with a touch of gray hair in his beard. The picture was just of his face, and what really stuck out to me were his eyes. They looked kind and suddenly, I started to feel a little better.

"Good morning Ms. Simmons." He stood up to greet me. His whole vibe was good so I shook his hand. "Or would you prefer for me to call you Jayla?"

"Jayla is good."

"You can have a seat." He pointed to the couch on the other side of him. Looking around the room it was your typical counseling office. There was a beautiful oak office desk and chair, a dark couch, a coffee table that had a box of tissues on it, and the comfortable chair that he sat in.

I sat down and settled myself. My heart was still racing, but not as much as it was before.

"So, what brings you in today?" he asked.

"I don't even know where to start."

"Start where you feel the most comfortable."

"I feel like I should start at the beginning before I start telling you about what has happened now."

"You tell me whatever you need to Jayla. I'm here for you."

When he said that, I felt more at ease. Slowly, I began to open up to Dr. Wood.

"I'm not from Houston. I was born and raised mostly on the Southside of Chicago. We lived in the hood."

"When you say 'we,' you are talking about your family?" he asked. I then noticed he had a notepad out. He was going to need more than that little bitty notepad to write what I had going on.

"Yes, me, my little brother, my little sister, my mother, and my father. My father was really into the street life. He was a drug dealer and that's how he paid the bills. He would buy us stuff and it was like his regular job. You know how some people get up in the morning and get to work? My father did the same. For so long it was normal to me." I paused. "Maybe it was normal to me because it was never really a secret what he was doing. It wasn't like it was hidden from us. We knew that Dad made his money from the streets. Maybe I knew more than my little brother and sister, but that's just how it was. That was our life until…" I stopped speaking.

"Until?" Dr. Wood pressed on.

"Until he was murdered when I was six years old."

The room was silent. I looked at his face trying to judge his reaction, but he really didn't have any. Had he heard worse shit than this?

"Tell me more."

"Well after he was murdered, my mother was never the same. From what I know, my mother and father were like soulmates or something. She knew what he was doing, but she loved him. That's why she stayed with him and had three kids by him. There was nothing that anybody could say that would make her leave my Dad. She loved him so much and when he died, she just changed."

"How did she change?"

"Before my father's death, my mother was the most loving woman you would ever meet. Yes, my father spoiled us by buying us things, but my mother spent all her time with us. She took us to the park, she took us everywhere. I can still remember her taking us to the zoo or to any amusement parks."

"She sounds as if she was hands on."

"She really was." I smiled thinking about the memories. "She really was the best Mom before that all happened. She changed so much."

I stopped for a minute. Dr. Wood looked at me, but he didn't say anything. I just nodded my head and took a deep breath.

"The change in my Mom started slow. I first thought it was because she had to start working now. She was never working before and she really didn't have any skills. She took any job she could get. She was a cashier, a maid, a babysitter, just anything so we could have some food on the table. She started to get tired and grumpy, and then something just switched. When I turned 10, I noticed that she didn't try to go to work anymore. She barely went grocery shopping unless I complained about there being no food in the house. Then when I was 12, I knew what it was. One day, I walked in her room to ask her about something, and I found beer bottles and liquor bottles everywhere. They were all empty and then I saw something else. On the floor there was needles and I just knew. I knew that my mother was now on drugs."

A tear slowly rolled down my eye just thinking about it. Speaking those words brought me back to her bedroom. The light coming in from the windows, the sound of me walking through the glass bottles, and that smell that damn near killed me. When I looked at my mother on the bed, she looked like a stranger to me.

"Take your time." Dr. Wood said. I realized I'd been sitting there silently in the room for some time. Reaching out to grab a tissue, I wiped my eyes.

"She wasn't my mother anymore after that day. There was no way the woman that let herself go like that, was the same woman that raised me." I cried softly. "I had to become a mother figure to both my little brother and sister when I was only 12 years old. Luckily, I had some family that helped me out here and there, but it was mostly me. I would steal to get food if we needed it and I started babysitting to make some money. It got to a point where I had to hide my money and my things so my mom wouldn't steal them. I worked so hard to get out of Chicago. My little sister was always good in school, so she went to private school and now she's in a really good college that is out of state. My little brother was giving me some trouble, but now he's turned his life around. I worked hard for that."

The tears came down some more, but they were happy tears. Thinking of how far I came made me proud. I wiped my face clean and chuckled.

"I've come so far."

"You sound surprised," Dr. Wood remarked. "Maybe finally saying it out loud has shown you what you're capable of."

"Yeah." I nodded. "You're right."

"Is there anything more you want to tell me? We still have more time left."

"I guess it's time to talk about why I'm really here."

My heartbeat was normal and that made me smile slightly. I felt nervous but not as much as before.

"After leaving Chicago, I moved to Atlanta. I took classes to become a CNA because I didn't want to be like my Mom. I didn't want to have no skills and not be able to get a job. While going to my CNA classes, I met my two best friends Charmaine and Kim. Charmaine is a hot mess but I love her. And Kim?" I chuckled. "Kim is so cool that you just automatically feel alright around her. I was making my own little life in Atlanta and then I met Darius." I stopped. the name felt weird to say and suddenly my heart started speeding up.

"Tell me more about Darius."

"Where do I begin?" I looked up at the ceiling. "Darius was a handsome man, he was a kind man, and I loved him. We met at a club and everything started out good. We were texting, and kissing, and having sex...just doing what typical couples do. I really thought that I'd found the one guy I was going to be with my whole life. Everything was going great Dr. Wood, but then I found out that he was married with a kid. I should have left him alone the second I found out. I should have left him be, but I was so in love with him that I couldn't stop. Plus he told me the typical married man lies about how he was going to leave his wife to be with me. For a moment, it looked like he really was going to do it, but then he was killed right outside of my house. He died in my arms." I looked down at my hands remembering all the blood that was there that night. "And I could never prove it, but I always had a feeling his wife had something to do with it."

A huge weight came off of my chest. It felt like it was a secret that I'd been holding in forever. Dr. Wood was still as cool as ice. Nothing seemed to make his facial expressions change much.

"And then there was Shane."

As soon as I said that, an alarm went off.

"Sadly, our time is up, but I do not have another appointment after you. If you want, you can stay here and talk about Shane. I have a feeling it's something you need to do." He brought up and I nodded. "So, tell me about Shane."

"Well, after everything that happened in Atlanta with Darius, I moved to Houston. I was just so afraid that I was going to die next. I for sure thought that his wife was going to come and get me or my family, so we all moved here. I liked it here and I was making sure to concentrate on work and my brother Keon, who lives with me. And for a while, that was good. I was still a little down about what happened with Darius, but the more time I spent here with new work and new friends, I felt better and better. I started going to the gym and hanging out with my friend, Samara. Samara is the one that introduced me to Shane because that's her brother. She was handsome too and super successful, but what I liked about him the most was the way that he treated me. He was always kind to me and from what I thought, he was honest. Honesty was very important to me, especially with what happened in Atlanta, but he withheld some things."

"What did he not tell you?"

I stopped to scratch my head a little bit. I

didn't know why I felt nervous, because I had done nothing wrong, but I guess a part of me felt ashamed.

"He didn't tell me that he had a kid and a crazy ass baby mama. Once I found that out, I should have left him," I told Dr. Wood. "I should have went running especially with all that I went through in Atlanta, but I didn't, and it only got worse."

"How did it get worse?" He asked me, but I couldn't speak. A minute or two later, he asked again. "Jayla, how did it get worse?" His voice was soft and understanding, but I still didn't say anything. "Take your time."

The palms of my hands started to get sweaty so I wiped it on my pants. My heart was racing and I took another deep breath. From the corner of my eye, I saw a small mini fridge. He must have saw me looking at it because he got up, opened it, and reached inside. He pulled out a small bottle of water. Without asking me, he handed it to me and I nodded. Quickly, I gulped down most of what I could. Tapping the side of the bottle, I felt ready to speak.

"Shane's baby mama was crazy." I told

him again. "Now this wasn't your typical crazy chick. She didn't call me up and curse me out, or hit me up on social media, Damiah would pop up at random places. She came to my job and started shit. She tried to fight me on more than once, and plus she threatened me all the time. She wanted me to *know* that Shane was still hers and that I should leave him alone. She warned me to not still date him and she finally kept true to her word. She held me hostage and tried to kill me."

It was only then when I spoke the words that I saw a change in Dr. Wood's face. His eyes got a little sad, but it didn't stay like that for long.

"I'm sorry to hear that."

"It's fine. She's in jail, along with her friend, and she's not coming out any time soon. Now Shane is raising his son by himself."

"I see." He started to scribble something on his page. He looked up at me.

"What?"

"You still haven't told me much about your relationship with Shane."

"What's there to say?"

"Do you not want to really talk about him?"

"I told you about his crazy baby mama."

"But that's about Damiah, and not him. Tell me about you and Shane."

The seconds passed by and I drank some more water. It wasn't that long before the whole bottle was empty. Tossing it in the empty wastebasket that was next to me, I decided it was time to speak.

"I love Shane. I want to say so bad that I'm not longer in love with him, but I do. How can I still be in love with someone whose drama almost killed me? I could have died, Dr. Wood." I leaned forward. "Do you understand? I could have died over some bullshit. And as much as I miss him, I can't go back there. I can't even think about Shane because all that I went through. Like, a huge part of me wants to reach out to him, but I can't because I know that I'm not ready."

The tears started flowing again, and this time it felt so good. Finally letting that part of me out felt powerful. Telling Kim was just the start.

"Jayla," Dr. Wood put his notepad down.

"I can tell that you're a very strong woman. You've been through a lot and still you want to do so much more. I commend you for all that you've done for not only yourself, but for your family. You've had to hold it down at a really young age and you did it really well. As far as your love life goes, you've taken on the same role there as well."

"What do you mean?"

"Well, with your mother's drug use, that made you take a responsibility you shouldn't have. You stepped up and claimed a role that you had no business doing. I get the situation, but you were just a child yourself. You had no business stepping up and doing what you did."

"But I had to."

"I get that, but you it wasn't your place. Just because you had to do it, doesn't mean it was your place. Do you understand what I mean?"

I agreed. I took on an adult role way too soon. Even though there was no choice, it still wasn't something a 12-year-old girl had to do. Someone should have been taking care of me.

"And now it seems you have adapted that role in your love life. You speak about Darius and his wife, but in a way you still take responsibility for a situation that seemed to go out of control. You still say of things of what you 'should have done,' but his murder was out of your control." He pointed out. "And even with Shane, you blame yourself for what has happened to you."

"But I should have left."

"Is that your crime? It's your fault for being essentially kept hostage and almost murdered?"

"No, of course not."

"But you speak as if it is." He brought up his notepad again. He flipped through some pages and then stopped. "Let me ask you this, if you'd known in the beginning about how dangerous Damiah was, would you have continued on dating Shane?"

"No." I answered quickly.

"Then why do you punish yourself as if you had all the knowledge in the world about Damiah?"

"Because as soon as I found out that Shane lied to me, I should have left."

"Do you think that Shane and Darius are the same person?"

Hearing that question blew me back. I tried to say that I didn't, but the words wouldn't come out. Maybe a part of me really did think that they were the same. I mean, both Shane and Darius withheld some truth from me and look how both situations turned out.

"Darius and Shane are two completely different people. Darius lied to you for his own good, and Shane, I believe, thought he was protecting you," he went on.

"Protecting me?"

"Well Darius had a wife that he was still having some relationship with, correct?"

"I believe so."

"But was Shane still involved with Damiah?"

"I don't think so." I stopped and tried to think a bit more. "No, because she never said that they were together, she just said that he was hers. Plus, his sister would have told me if she thought they were together. I really think that all of this was in her head."

"And maybe Shane knew that. Maybe he was trying to protect you from her."

"But why not tell me about his son?"

"How can you tell you about his son without bringing up Damiah?"

Out of nowhere, a long breath of air came out of me. I felt myself just release.

"Right."

"Now, I believe that he could have handled that much better. Perhaps he could have told you the truth from the beginning, but there's no point in arguing that. Sadly, what has happened has already happened. We can't try to pick apart the past with hopes that we can change it; that's impossible."

"It is."

"What we can do is move forward. Shane, from what you've told me, seems like a good man. It also seems that you and he had a good relationship and that you both really cared for each other."

"We did."

"It's just sad that his past couldn't let him go. But know that the actions of Damiah are not his nor your responsibility."

"Should I reach out to Shane?"

"I would advise you not to. I think right now you have a lot of resentment and hurt, and that's normal given the circumstances."

He put his notepad down. "But you have to learn how to assign the hurt and resentment to the right people. Shane did not hurt you, Damiah and Darius did."

I was now nodding my head like crazy. Dr. Wood was speaking some gospel truth right now.

"Do not reach out to Shane right now until you finish working on yourself. If you were to reach out to him, it wouldn't be coming from the right place. If you want to, I'd like to continue working on this with you. We'll work on getting you to a place where you can push past the hurt, past the pain, and in a place where you can truly stand on your feet. It's time for you to take care of you."

I agreed and he gave me a reassuring smile. After that, I made sure to book multiple appointments with him. This appointment was exactly what I needed. Walking out the building, I felt great and I knew that this was only the beginning.

CHAPTER 4

Jayla

It had been three months since my first session with Dr. Wood and things had been going great. I'd been going to work when I was supposed to, without taking any days off. I'd also been taking walks to clear my head and had found a gym that Shane didn't own. Some days, I would go there with Crystal or Keon, but most days, like today, I went by myself.

I was on the treadmill walking at first, I started jogging and tried to build myself up to running. I wanted to beat my record for running for about three minutes straight. I picked up a lot of speed and just as I reached three minutes, I started to slow down. When I finished, I drank some water and stood by the machine. While trying to catch my breath, I looked around the gym. It was an early Saturday morning, so the gym wasn't that full. I finished off my water bottle when I noticed someone walking in.

This tall, muscular, brown skin brother walked in and stole all of my attention. He had a mustache, nice tight curls in his short haircut, that was cut off at the side like old school Will Smith. He was so good looking that I found myself staring at him. His body was like a basketball player's. He had muscles, but not that many. He wore this black tank that showed off his body. He was so sexy and I couldn't take my eyes off of him. He walked in and waved at the receptionist and suddenly we caught eyes.

It felt like we were looking at each other for a minute. He smiled at me and I felt myself blushing. He licked his hips and nodded at me, but that just made me look away. I giggled to myself a little bit and that shocked me. I definitely didn't have time for this. I had to concentrate on myself, but he was just so handsome, I couldn't help it. I popped my headphones in my ears, started listening to some music, and made my way to the elliptical. After an hour on the elliptical, I started to feel thirsty, so I decided to treat myself to an all-natural juice.

Looking over the menu, I was trying to think of what I wanted. Suddenly, I felt that someone was looking over at me. I followed that feeling and saw that the sexy guy that I was looking at earlier was looking right at me. I felt myself blush but went back to looking at the menu. After some time, I ordered the lemon and apple juice.

"What an interesting choice," a deep voice said from behind me. I didn't have to turn around to know who it was. His voice was just as sexy as everything else about him. I turned my head slightly and looked him up and down. His body was so nice but the fact that it has little sweat beads rolling down made him look even better. He didn't even smell bad either. He still had a scent of deodorant and some expensive cologne. Before I could talk to him, the person behind the counter handed me my juice.

"Thank you." I thanked her and moved off to the side.

In this gym, there were some tables were people could sit and drink their juices or smoothies. A few seconds later, he stood next to the table.

"Would you mind if I sat down?" he asked me, looking right into my eyes. Just him staring at me made me feel like we were all alone in this gym.

"Sure." I pointed to the seat opposite of me.

"I didn't want to bother you any more than I already have," he commented as he sat down.

"You aren't bothering me."

"Really?" He smiled. "I thought I was when you ignored me earlier."

"No, it's not that. I just got the juice back and forgot to say anything."

"Oh, are we going to blame it on the juice person now?" He laughed.

"No." I started giggling.

"What if I told you that you hurt my feelings when you played me like that?"

"So now you're saying that I played you?"

"Yup, you hurt my feelings."

We both started laughing. It was weird how natural this felt.

"My name is Kamel." He reached out his hand.

"Jayla." I told him, but I didn't give my hand to him.

"You see? You keep trying to play me," he joked. "Why wouldn't you give me your hand?"

"I don't know. It just felt kind of corny," I teased.

"Oh...you know how to cut a man deep." He pretended to pass out on the table. "I'm dead."

"You'll be alright."

"Are you sure? What if when I go home, I die because you cut me so deep? How will you ever know?"

"I don't know." I shrugged my shoulders.

"How about we exchange numbers? You know, just to check up on each other."

"Okay." I surprisingly answered as we slid our phones to each other.

Kamel and I talked some more before we

both tossed our empty cups of juice in the garbage.

"So, what if I told you that I wanted to take you out?" We were by the exit.

"I don't know about that."

"Why? You got a boyfriend or husband or something?"

"No." I shook my head. "But I just got out of something and I'm trying to be about me right now."

"I'm trying to be about you too." He laughed and I playfully pushed him. "Okay, I won't push you to do anything you don't want to do. I just hope I get the chance to have dinner or lunch with you. But if I'm lucky, I'll get to bump into you again."

"I'll think about that dinner date."

"Promise?" He smiled and I felt myself melt just a little bit.

"Promise."

"I can't wait."

I headed out the gym towards my car. Looking back at the gym, I saw Kamel wave at me before he walked back inside. Butterflies flew all around in my stomach. What are the chances that I would meet someone so sexy like Kamel? I guess Kim was right, I just needed to get back to doing things for me.

When I got home I took a shower and started to unwind for the day. I decided on some Netflix and chill with myself. There was this show I was trying to catch up on. Keon was at his job placement program. They were trying him out as a pharmacy tech in various locations to see if they could find the right fit. With him gone, I had the whole house to myself. I grabbed some fruit, got on the couch in my sweats, and turned on the program. Hours later, I must have fallen asleep, because soon, I felt Keon tapping me.

"You got knocked out," he said in his Chris Tucker voice. "You snoring and everything."

"Shut up." I softly punched him. "I do not snore."

"Either you snoring or we got some wild animals in the house." He started laughing.

"That's not funny Keon." I stuck out my tongue at him.

"Whatever." He plopped down on the couch. "What were you watching anyway?"

"Well it's a show about two friends who fall in love—"

"Ugh, don't need to hear it." He rolled his eyes. "Wait a minute, what are you doing watching love stories?"

"What do you mean?"

"Usually you'll watch like a documentary or some show, but you never really watch some lovey-dovey shit. What's going on?"

"What?" I tried to not smile, but I couldn't help it.

"Come on Sis, you know you can't hide anything from me."

"Fine."

I broke down and told my brother all about Kamel. He nodded his head while listening to the story and when I finished he spoke.

"I think that's a good thing."

"You do? You don't think I'm moving too fast?"

"Too fast?" He stopped to laugh for a second.

"What's so funny?"

"Jayla, you are single. You can do what

you want. You can date this guy if you want to."

"Even after everything?"

"Yeah." He shrugged his shoulders. He got up and headed towards his room, but he stopped. "Just do me a favor though."

"What is that?"

"Don't go falling in love so quick."

I reached behind me and threw my pillow at him. He caught it laughing and tossed it back.

"I'm just saying, don't go picking out wedding dresses or nothing."

"Whatever Keon, I'm not that soft. I can keep my feelings in check."

"Please." He laughed out loud but then he stopped. "But seriously, I think it's a good idea."

"You do?"

"Yeah, besides you got to eat."

"Oh really?" I started laughing. "I thought dudes hated to be used for free meals."

"Come on Jayla, it's all a part of the game. You can just go out with him and have a nice time."

"Okay." I agreed.

Later that night, my phone buzzed. To my surprise, it was a text message from Kamel.

"Hey. How you doing tonight?" he asked. I started to giggle and I shook my head that he could make me feel like this.

"I'm good," I sent back.

"Wow. That's all I get? You stay trying to play me." He added a laughing face at the end.

"You're so sensitive," I joked.

"Nah not really, you just like to break my heart sweetheart. But let me stop playing games. How are you? I was thinking about you."

I chuckled and shook my head. As much as I hate to admit it, I miss the attention I use to get from men. I've been keeping myself so closed off after everything happened, I forgot how good it could feel for a sexy guy to be interested in you. Kamel and I kept texting throughout the whole night. It wasn't until I looked at the clock and saw that it was one in the morning did I notice how much we texted.

"Damn we been texting for hours," I sent him. "I got to go to sleep."

"You got a bedtime?"

"No, big head, I don't."

"Well that's good because that gives me just enough time to ask you out for dinner."

Unlike the other text messages he sent me, I didn't answer this one right away. It had been so long since I went on a date. The last date I had was with Shane. I felt my nerves come back so I took a deep breath. I got quiet and tried to think of what the words would the counselor say? If Dr. Woods were in this room with me, what would he suggest? He probably would tell me in a soft voice to just go ahead.

"We can go out to dinner."

"Dinner sometime soon? Is that good?"

"That's fine."

I leaned back into my sofa. My nerves were going crazy but I think I was mostly excited. Even though I haven't been out since Shane, maybe this change could be a good thing.

A couple days passed since I met Kamel and we were still texting each other back and forth. When I was at work and I had some time to myself, I was texting him. I was trying to be careful to not text him in front of Samara because I didn't want her to know yet.

We still hadn't really talked about Shane since the trial. I didn't want her to feel weird now that I was talking to someone else.

"Guess what?" Kamel texted me around lunch.

"What?" I asked.

"I'm around your job. I was in the area handling business."

"Oh ok."

"Don't think I'm trying to stalk you okay. I was really here for business."

"I never thought that." I chuckled because I knew how much Kamel liked to joke around.

"Good because I would like to take you out for lunch."

My heart started beating fast, but it stopped when I realized that I actually liked Kamel. Not only was he sexy, but we actually got along. If I told myself that I was going to try new things, then one of them had to be letting Kamel take me out on dates.

"Sure, where would you like to meet?"

Ten minutes later I was pulling up my car to this trendy cafe. How could I never have seen this place before? It looked like a mixture of a log cabin and the future. Almost everything was wood, but the lights were something you'd see in those movies or tv shows about the future. All the people that worked there wore nice shirts and pants. It was so cool.

"Hey," Kamel said next to me. He smelled so sexy and looked so good wearing some business slacks and button up shirt.

"Oh, so you were really working?" I teased.

"I told you I wasn't stalking you, but if I was, I wouldn't admit it," he joked and I laughed. "What's up? How are you?"

"I'm good, but I feel like I should have changed out my clothes. I took off the shirt, but left the pants on."

"It doesn't matter because you still look beautiful. You could come out here rocking a potato sack and you'd still be the most beautiful woman in the room."

"That was kind of smooth," I complimented him. He smiled and opened the entrance door for me.

"I'm not the smooth kind of guy. I just speak from the heart and I like what I like."

We sat in the cafe and one of the waiters came right over to us. He handed us a bottle of water and told us he would be back with the menu. Within seconds he came back and we ordered our food. Taking a look around the cafe, I could see why a lot of people liked to hang out here. It had this chill vibe to it. There was old school R&B playing in the background. People were chatting with each other, swaying to the music, or they were just eating. The people that worked there were extremely cool and nice.

"You like my choice?" Kamel asked.

"Yeah, you have pretty good taste," I gave him a compliment. "I've been to this neighborhood before, but I don't think I've ever noticed this place.

"Oh yeah, it's so laid back that it doesn't stand out. You kinda have to know people to know about this place."

"Do you know those kind of people?" I questioned him.

"I make sure I make the right connections. I'm all about keeping the important people in my life," he answered with a smile.

"I see." I blushed.

The whole lunch went really well. He made me feel so comfortable, but on top of all of that, he was so funny. He had me cracking up the whole time. Even when the waiter came over, he left the table chuckling too. It was cool to be with someone that everyone felt comfortable being around.

"So, what made you decide to come out to lunch with me?" he asked out of nowhere as we were finishing lunch.

"I don't know. Why do you ask that?"

"I don't know, it just seems like you didn't want to hang out with me."

"Are you going to start saying that I curved you again?"

"I told you, I'm sensitive."

"Well don't cry on me now; that would be crazy awkward."

"But what if I gave you that man cry?"

"Ugh, don't tell me you believe in thug tears too?"

"Thug tears?"

"You know, when one tear slide down your face and that's it."

"Well I didn't choose the thug life, it chose me," he joked and we started to crack up.

Lunch was fun and it sucked when my

alarm went off on my phone. I told Kamel it was time for me to get back to work.

"Well, it's not like I could keep you all to myself." He grinned. We walked to the exit and started making our way to our car.

"Thanks for lunch," I told him.

"It's not a problem, Jayla." His sexy voice sounded so good saying my name. "I'm just glad you didn't try to curve me," he joked.

"Never that."

"Oh yeah?"

Within seconds, he looped his arm around my lower back, and gently pulled me in for a kiss. It took me by surprise but what shocked me more was the fact I put one of my arms around his neck. His grip on my body felt so right and the butterflies in my stomach started flying like crazy. When he let me go, I could feel a small goofy smile grow across my face.

"I'll talk to you later," he told me and I couldn't even speak. I watched him walk to his car and soon I got into mine. We both drove off in separate directions. On the drive back to work, I still had that goofy smile on my face. I felt pretty lucky, but only time would tell.

CHAPTER 5

Shane

It was time for the meeting with the board of investors. I brought them all down to discuss the new building for the gym and how I plan on expanding the business. We had daycares, juice bars, and small cafes in some of our gyms. Now I was proposing that we'd have licensed masseuses and great chiropractors. I was slowly trying to turn my gyms more into a spa. I was picturing bringing in a whole new clientele and I needed my investors in on this. Although I'd more than reached the point where I could invest in it myself, there was nothing like having their finances to do it with.

My assistant walked in and placed all the packets on the conference tables. Each packet had all the numbers about the gym expansion. She then came back in and had the caterers set up the brunch on the other side of the room. No one likes making decisions on an empty stomach. Finally, Tone walked in with the investors and I personally shook each hand. When everyone was settled and seated, I started my presentation. After ten minutes of going over my plans, showing them possible pictures of the gym expansion, and even meeting some of the masseuses, all the investors agreed to hand over more money. It wasn't that long before we were all eating brunch.

"You did it again." Tone walked into my office bringing in a plate from brunch.

"I'm surprised you didn't say behind with the investors in the conference room."

"What? Did you think you're the only one that wants some alone time?" he joked as he sat down. "So, what's been going on with you?"

"What do you mean?"

"I know you've been taking care of little man, how's that going?"

"You know, I won't even lie to you. At first, it was kind of hard because of all the shit that went down with Damiah. She might have been fucking crazy when it came to me, but she was a good mother to my son. I'm never going to take that away from her. I can see she was a good Mom because my son just talks about her all the time. It was hard to hear about that at first."

Tone nodded his head, but I knew he had no real way of understanding what I meant. To be honest, I still was having a hard time understanding everything and it was my life. It had been six months since I've seen Jayla and all I'd been doing is work and my son. Luckily I had my family to help; especially my sister Samara, or I would be going crazy. She always came over if I needed her, gave me some tips, and of course watched her nephew whenever she could.

"I know shit must be crazy because you're all about work now," Tone spoke up. "It's like I hardly see you."

"What are you talking about? I see you at work every day," I pointed out.

"Nah, but we haven't gone out in such a long time."

"I know, but you know what I'm going through. I don't got time to be out there with you in the clubs."

"Man, you sound like some old lady right now."

"Dang, why I got to be an old lady though? You couldn't make me an old man?" I laughed, almost choking on my orange juice.

"Nah, because old men still go to clubs."

We both started cracking up. Just then my assistant came in and said that the investors wanted to see me. I stepped out briefly, spoke to the investors, and then sent them on their way. Within days I would be signing new contracts. When I came back into my office, Tone was leaning back in his chair.

"Don't fall asleep here," I warned. "I'm not trying to hear you snore."

"Man, you a hater." He sat up straight. "Everything cool?"

"Yeah the papers will be put in soon. We can get started on the expansion right away.

I'm thinking we can maybe start a little early. How about later in day we go scope out that building we had in mind?"

"Damn, can we chill and fall back?"

"Why? We can get started on it right now."

"Look, you my boy, and I know you've been busy with your son and work, but you need to chill. Take a break."

"I don't need a break."

"What you talking about? Everyone needs a break. You've been working like crazy so you need one too. I mean, what you up to tonight?"

"I just told you. I'm going to look up the building for the gym's expansion."

"Come on. It's Friday. We used to go out on Fridays, remember?"

I knew what Tone was trying to do, but a part of me didn't want to hear it. Without Jayla, I really didn't want to go out. Even though it was six months, I still thought about her, but maybe Tone was right. Maybe I had to get a night out to put everything behind me.

"Okay, so what do you have planned?"

"Oh, you serious? You not gonna make up some more excuses or nothing?"

"Shut up." I threw a paper ball at him. "I said I'm going, so what's the plan?"

"Why don't we do what we use to do? Let's hit the club or something. Maybe we can go to a bar."

"I guess."

"Don't try to sound enthusiastic or nothing."

"Whatever, let me ask my sister if she can watch my son tonight."

"Yeah, call your fine ass sister. She got them curves…" He had a silly smile on his face.

"Shut up before I beat your ass." I jokingly raised my hand like I was going to pimp smack him.

Samara picked up the phone on the third ring.

"What's going on bro? How did the whole meeting go?"

"It went good. I sealed the deal and everything is going to go as planned."

"I'm happy to hear that. You should be out celebrating right now."

"Well that's what Tone was saying, but I didn't know if you could watch your nephew tonight. I know it's last minute—"

"Boy you already know that I got you. I love my nephew and he loves me. We'll have a huge sleepover."

"Thank you so much. I appreciate everything that you do."

"Oh, don't be so sappy." I knew she was rolling her eyes. "Do me a favor and leave some money for some take out because I'm not cooking anything. Also, get me a bottle of wine."

"Well damn, is there anything else that you need? What else do you want me to do?"

"I'm gonna need you to be careful of the thotties out there. You might get caught up." She started cracking up. I laughed along with her and shook my head.

"I'm a grown ass man. I know how to handle myself."

"Surrrrre," she scoffed. "Whatever you say. Look, I'll go pick up the kids from the daycare, take them, and have fun at my house."

"Thanks sis and call me if you need anything."

Later that night, Tone and I rolled up to the bar that's in downtown Houston. It had to be packed because there was a line outside. Tone walked up to the bouncer and we were let in right away. People knew us around Houston. We used to run the scene back in the day. Tone and I use to have ladies, liquor, and money wherever we went. Our reputation back in the day was crazy. We threw money around everywhere when the gyms first started to pop off. I was glad we grew up from that.

"Damn this place is jumping." Tone said while we took some seats. "It's like a club in here."

"I see that." There were people everywhere just eating, drinking, and vibing out to the music. The whole place was huge but still there were a lot of people inside. "And more people want to come inside."

"Aren't you glad you came out here?"

"Yeah I guess so."

"Stop lying." He bumped into me with his shoulder. "Look around at all this talent."

I turned around and saw all the beautiful

women. There were tall, skinny, thick, black, white, Latina, Asian, just a whole mix of women. Some of them came up to us and tried to talk to us. Tone, of course, was taking down numbers and social media information before he sent them away. I wasn't really feeling them. These ladies were just throwing themselves at me and it just made me feel a way.

A light skin woman with curly hair sat next to me. She had on a black tank, a tutu, and some red high heeled shoes. Her outfit was a bit crazy, but she was cute and she pulled it off. She had a nice size ass and breasts, so even her body was on point. She immediately ordered a drink and turned to me and Tone.

"How are you guys doing?" she asked both of us but was looking right at me.

"We're good," Tone answered. "What's up with you?"

"I'm good. I just thought that you were looking at little lonely." Again she was looking right at me.

"Lonely, huh?" I nodded my head and sipped my drink slowly. "What makes you think that?"

"Just look at you. You should have a fine lady on your arm."

"Oh, I should?"

"Yeah." She blinked slowly at me. "Am I pretty enough to be that lady for you?"

"You're gorgeous," I told her truthfully.

"Thank you. I actually model."

"Oh, you do runway?"

"No."

"Fashion?"

"No." She got a little quieter.

"Then what do you model?"

She smiled at me and reached in her phone. She pulled up her Instagram account and showed me her profile.

"I got over 30,000 followers." She smiled broadly. She had mostly half naked pictures and she looked good, but her thirst was turning me off. She kept telling me more and more of how guys hit her up, her celebs wanted her in her videos, and all these other things trying to impress me. I didn't care about none of that, but she didn't get the clue. She just kept going on and on about how she loved to go out, and how she loved to drink. I started to drown her out, but it wasn't until she started talking about fitness that I knew what she was really trying to say.

"So, you like to work out?" I asked her and she nodded. "You go to gyms?" I asked and she gave me a knowing look. "How long did you know that I owned a line of gyms?"

"You do?" Her acting skills were horrible.

"Come on shorty, you already knew that." Tone butted in the conversation, laughing. "Everyone knows that. His damn face is on all the billboards and advertisements." Me and him both started laughing. "If you want to be the face of the company, why not just say that?"

Tone and I were both use to ladies throwing themselves at us because of our money. They tried to get at us any way they could. This lady might have been saying she wanted to be our fitness model, but the fact that she didn't tell us at first let us know that she was trying to get at me for the money. She looked embarrassed as Tone asked her typical fitness model questions because she couldn't answer any. I just shook my head, told her to apply on the website, and turned away.

"Let's not let that ruin tonight," Tone

leaned over and said to me. He must have read it on my face that I was getting ready to leave. I wanted to be done. I was not used to this anymore. My life was in a whole different direction.

"I'm not." I lied but slowly I was trying to think of an excuse to why we had to leave. Before I could speak, a thick chocolate woman passed us by. She had a medium sized waist but huge tits and ass. I quickly shot a look at Tone. This was definitely his type of woman. He was staring at her as she passed us by. She gave Tone a shy smile and walked to the other side of the bar.

I snapped my finger in his face to snap him out of it.

"What?" He tried to play it off.

"You about to stare a hole into that woman," I joked.

"Nah…" He shrugged his shoulders.

"Go holla at her," I told him.

"We came out to hang together." He was looking at her.

"Man…" I gave him a soft nudge towards her.

"Well, I'm not going to let you bring me down."

"What?"

"You over here frontin' like none of these ladies is banging." He started to get up. "I'm going to enjoy myself." He walked over to her.

"I bet you will," I called after him shaking my head.

Tone was with the female for about five minutes and I felt like I had to leave. I couldn't fake it anymore. I wanted to just go home, work on the presentation, and then crash. I didn't want to be here for long. I got up, ready to find Tone and tell him that I was gone, when I saw someone. She was gorgeous. She had neat braids, pretty eyes, a tight dress that hugged her body, and all the guys staring at her. Guys were coming up to her but she kept turning them down. Every one of them, she told them that she wasn't interested. I didn't know why, but I started walking to her. I guess I was one who was always up for a challenge.

"Is anybody sitting here?" I asked her pointing to the seat next to her.

"No, but I kinda want to leave it there for my purse." She didn't even look at me. She must have been used to all type of guys coming up to her, so she wasn't in the mood.

"Oh, come on. Your purse is more important than me?" I said with a smile and I saw her turn to look at me. She had an attitude on her face for only a second. Soon as she saw me, I saw her whole personality change. "Now, can I sit down?"

"If you want." She flirted with me a little bit. "Sorry about before."

"Yeah, you damn near cut my head off." I laughed.

We sat down and had a pretty good time. Her name was Nicole and she was a corporate lawyer for a financial company. I was pretty impressed and when I told her about my company, she was impressed too.

"I can't imagine what your day-to-day is like." She ordered us both drinks. "I know it's more than just picking out gym equipment."

"Naturally. It's a lot of meetings and trying to find out how to get the business to grow," I informed her. "What about you?"

"Being a corporate lawyer is as exciting as it sounds." We both started to chuckle. "It's nothing but fun and laughter all the time."

She shook her head. "But honestly, it's nothing but paperwork and maybe once in a while a meeting. We do have corporate getaways, but that's about it. But I love it." She smiled. "And despite all the hard work, I wouldn't trade none of it."

Nicole was definitely a classy woman. She knew how to carry herself and she knew the importance of hard work. Even though she thought her job was boring, she still was going to stick by it.

Hours passed and it was time to go. I glanced around the bar looking for Tone, but he was long gone. I checked my phone and saw that he texted earlier saying he was leaving with the woman from earlier. I should have known.

"Well, I got a long day tomorrow," she told me, standing up, and we started walking towards the exit.

"It's the weekend," I pointed out.

"You say that as if that means something." She laughed. "You already know I barely have any days off. There's this huge case coming up so I have to use any time that I have."

"I feel you, I have this expansion coming up so, I get it."

"That's good." We stood in front of the exit and she pointed across the parking lot. "My car is over there."

"I'll walk you over there."

"No, that's okay."

"I'm sorry, but that's not how I roll."

I walked her to her car. Before she got inside, we exchanged numbers. She started to drive away, honked twice, and she was out. I guess Tone was right. I should try to relax more often.

CHAPTER 6

Jayla

It was time for my appointment with Dr. Wood. When the receptionist called me in, I didn't feel nervous. It had been months of this and I still was going every week. It got to the point that I needed to see Dr. Wood. It became necessary because I was no longer holding anything in. When I saw Dr. Wood it was to get everything off my chest.

"How are you doing Jayla?" He greeted me as soon as I walked in the room.

"I'm okay." I sighed and sat down.

"Just okay?" he asked and the look in his eyes told me he wanted to know more.

"Yeah, I'm doing okay."

"Is there something you want to share?"

"Well... I met this guy some time back and I think I like him."

"You think?"

"I don't want to say that I like him for real just yet."

"Why not?"

"I'm just afraid."

"Jayla, we've been through this."

Dr. Wood had been telling me in most of my sessions that I couldn't let the past mess up my future, but that was easier said than done. I looked at Kamel, who was so sexy and funny, and all I could think of was Shane and Darius. Would he be like them too?

"I know Dr. Wood and I'm trying not to judge him but—"

"But nothing Jayla." His voice was always steady. "Tell me more about this young man."

"His name is Kamel and I met him at the gym. He's very good looking and so funny. Like every time we text or talk, I'm always laughing. He's so cool to be around and it's nice. With Shane it was like that too, but

Kamel makes me laugh even more than Shane ever did."

"Well that sounds good. I think you should go out with him."

"We had lunch a while back."

"And how was that?"

"It was good and we had a…" I paused and closed my eyes. I felt Kamel's arm around my waist and his soft lips touching mine. "We had a kiss at the end."

"Sounds like you had a good time."

"It is."

"So, what's holding you back?"

"I don't know if I'm ready. Keon says that I should just have a few dates with him, but don't get into anything serious."

"I would have to agree with Keon, he's right. You can just date and have fun with him. You don't need to be mentally picturing your future with him or anything like that. You can just socialize."

"So, you're suggesting that I get with him?"

"I'm suggesting that you have fun."

To hear Dr. Wood agree with Keon was the last thing that I thought would happen. I thought for sure he would have said that I had to slow down and not date at all.

"So, tell me about Shane? Have you tried to reach out to him?"

"No, but every now and then, I think about it."

"What stops you from contacting him?"

"I just want to focus on me right now. I can't even think about him without thinking about Damiah. I just don't think it would be fair to contact him when I still can't separate him from her."

"That seems fair."

"As much as I want to contact him, I think that I should just move on."

"Hmm." He brought out another note pad. "I have to say, you've made tremendous leaps with your counseling. You can now mention Shane and Damiah without getting angry and now you're being considerate when it comes to Shane. I'm proud of how far you've come. I think you're ready to truly tackle your love life. Whether you try it out with Kamel, get back with Shane, or try someone entirely new, you're ready now. You're truly ready to date."

The session continued and Dr. Wood just kept telling me that I was doing well. I really needed to hear that, and I also needed to hear that I should still pursue Kamel. I think I really needed to give dating a real shot.

~

Shane

I PULLED up to the restaurant, trying go see if I could spot Nicole's car. Since I met her the other day, we texted back and forth. With both of our schedules being so crazy, we finally settled on a time and place for us to meet. Tone was so excited for me to go out, you'd think it was his date too. But I guess in his head he was trying to see me move on from Jayla. I didn't have to tell him that a big part of the reason why I didn't really go out was because I did miss Jayla. I missed her a lot, but there was nothing I could do. If she didn't want to talk to me., I had to respect that.

Finally I spotted her all white Range Rover pulling up. She halfway honked her horn and waved at me. After parking and turning her car off, she stepped out. She looked gorgeous in her backless white short dress. I couldn't stop staring at her legs. She had these thick thighs and there's something about thick thighs that just turn me into an idiot.

"Sorry. I hope you weren't waiting long," she apologized and then gave me a hug. "Just trying to wrap up some things at work."

"It's okay. Trust me, I understand." I was trying not to stare at her thighs, but they were just calling me.

"Good." She took my hand and started leading me in. "Shall we go in?"

The restaurant was just as luxurious as it was in the pictures. I couldn't even get a good look around because I was still looking at her thighs. When she wasn't paying attention, I got another eyeful.

"Table for two?" The hostess asked and she prepared to bring us there, but Nicole stopped her.

"Please make sure it is one of the best tables in the house. I don't need a table anywhere near the bathroom and I don't need it to be crowded by a bunch of people. I

require privacy and attentive waiters, is that clear?"

The hostess looked stunned and then slid her gaze over to me. I was just in shock as she was. Pretty soon, the hostess brought us to a table. Nicole gave her a nod of approval and we both sat down. That situation turned me off for a second, but I let it slide. I had to remember that Nicole was an attorney. She was used to calling the shots and running the show. Her mind was probably still on lawyer mode.

"So, how was your day?" she asked me.

"It was busy, but that's the usual. The expansion of the gym is going very well. Not only did we land a great location, but I'm excited about the new employees. I think it will be very successful."

"I don't doubt it." She gave me a smile, but it seemed fake. She just didn't seem to care about what I said.

"How about you?"

"Work is work." She shrugged her shoulders. "But enough about that." She waved me off. "We didn't come here to talk about work."

"No, we didn't." I smiled, agreeing with her. "Let's get to know each other."

"What's there to know?" She had this seductive look on her face. "We're both adults who work hard and should be able to play hard too."

I was silent for a while because I truly had no response for her. I wanted to ask her what she meant by that statement, but soon the waiter came over and asked us for our orders. Before I could speak, she strongly suggested that I had something light. When I asked her why, she said that she didn't want us to waste our time eating. The more she spoke to me, the more I realized that the night we met was just me being drunk. There was nothing really special about her. On one hand she wasn't like the thirsty girls who are looking for a come up, but on the other hand, she was just boring. There was nothing about her that was attractive anymore. When she got up to use the bathroom, her thighs didn't even turn me on anymore. While she was gone, I decided this date was going to be cut short because I didn't plan on wasting anymore of my time.

Nicole came back to the table. It was hard

to believe how someone who was so attractive days before was now so ordinary to me.

"So, do you think that you can get yourself a plate to go?" she asked as soon as she sat down.

"Is there an emergency? Do you need to leave?" I sounded concerned, but in reality, I couldn't wait to go.

"No, that's not it at all. I just thought with us being two consenting adults, that there is no reason for us to pretend."

"Pretend?" I was confused. "What do you mean?"

"Let's not act like we want to get to know each other. We're not here looking for soulmates and we're not trying to get married. We should wrap this up and go back to my place. Are you going to get in my car or follow me there?"

That's when it all hit me. She was trying to get me to her house right away. I chuckled a little bit. This was a funny role reversal. She was like a thirsty dude that tried to take females home two seconds into a date. Now I knew what Samara meant. She used to joke that she didn't even get to enjoy her meal before her date was hinting that he wanted to take her home. I looked down at my plate. Most of my food was still there. My wine was untouched. I held back laughter and shook my head. This date was over.

Nicole kept talking. She couldn't tell that the whole mood was gone. She was still flirting and trying to get me to go home with her. I just nodded my head and sipped some of my wine. This date was done, but I was going to at least finish my meal. I wasn't going to box it up and then reheat it when I get home all because of her. But with her talking more and more, I couldn't even enjoy my food. I signaled for the waiter to come over. I was going to box it up after all, and have this for lunch. She ruined my appetite and I just wanted to get out of there. Before the waiter came over, I noticed something in the background. I squinted harder trying to make sure I was seeing everything correctly. Wow.

CHAPTER 7

Jayla

Tonight was the big dinner date with Kamel. Even though we went out to lunch already, for some reason this date felt like the first date. I was so nervous that I must have went through seven outfits just trying to find the right one. It had to be something nice because I still haven't forgiven myself for him seeing me in my work uniform pants. He said I was cute, but I didn't care. How I looked tonight has to erase the entire memory with that uniform on.

I went through every color of the rainbow until I landed on purple strapless dress. It was sexy dress, with a train, and a long slit. I spun around in the mirror a few times because I couldn't believe how good I looked. I completed it all with some black heels, diamond earrings, and my hair up in a neat bun. At the last minute, I added some makeup just to add a little bit of extra.

"Yaaaas," I told myself as I did a small twerk in front of the mirror.

Just then, my phone started vibrating and I snapped out of my little dance session. I saw Kamel's number and answered.

"I just finished getting dressed," I told him before he could even say hello.

"Mmm, I bet your ass looking sexy too."

"Maybe I should send you a picture," I teased, but I was somewhat serious about the offer.

"Only if you send it to my Snapchat."

"Snapchat?" I scrunched my face. "Why?"

"Oh, don't pretend that you don't like using those filters." We both started laughing. "You don't need any of them tho." He had me blushing and I haven't even seen him yet. "But, I was calling you to tell you to get ready. I'm down the block from your house. I'm going to be pulling up soon."

"Okay, I'll go outside right now."

After we hung up, I took one last look in the mirror. I looked perfect and I felt so sexy. Stepping out my house, I saw that Kamel just pulled in. He drove an all-white Rolls Royce. It was a good look and I was lowkey impressed, but I couldn't let him know. I was sure driving in that car, he'd gotten attention from all types of females, and I didn't want to come off thirsty. Besides, I was attracted to Kamel before I even knew what he drove.

"Damn, I had a feeling you were looking sexy, but I didn't think that you were looking *this* sexy." He stepped out his car. "I need to get a full visual of this." He took my hand softly and spun me around. "Sheesh." He laughed. "You are going to make this evening hard for me." He looked me up and down one more time. "All puns intended." We both laughed. Kamel could always crack me up within seconds of speaking to him. He walked over to the passenger side of his car. He opened the door. "Are you ready?"

I got in and saw him still staring at me.

"Shouldn't you be closing the door?" I asked, giggling.

"I can't help it." He sighed. "You look stunning." He had me blushing again. "You about to have me skip like a little kid." He closed the door and did a playful half skip. I started laughing out loud.

"You are the most," I told him when he got in the driver's seat. "I know you didn't just skip out there."

"I technically didn't skip. I did like a little manly hop." He winked. "It was super masculine," he said in a superhero voice.

"Oh my goodness." I shook my head. "Where are you taking me? You didn't tell me where we were going, so I took a chance and dressed like this."

"Two things." He turned and looked right in my eyes. "One: you made the right choice with that outfit."

"And what is the other thing?"

"It's a surprise where I'm taking you."

"Ugh, come on. I'm not five years old, you can tell me where we're going."

"Where's the fun in that?" he snickered.

"Can't I just get a clue?"

"Of course." He had a huge smile on his face. "The clue is, we can eat there."

"Not even a little clue." I batted my eyelashes at him playfully.

"You're sexy and all, but that's not going to work." He laughed a little more and looked back at the road.

"Well am I at least dressed right for the place?"

"Enough with the twenty questions." He chuckled. "Just trust me."

"Yes sir!" I gave him a captain's salute. "But all I know you better not be dragging me to McDonald's or Twin Peaks or anything like that, because I'll beat your ass."

"I got you," he promised.

After a few minutes of him driving we pulled up to this beautiful restaurant. The place looked familiar and I was trying to think of where I've seen this place before. I finally realized that this was the restaurant that a lot of celebrities went to. I had seen this place so many times on reality shows and on magazines, but I'd never been inside. I read that it was almost impossible to get into without a reservation because of all the celebs and the very best of Houston going here.

"What do you do?" I asked him because it

occurred to me that I never asked him before. I just thought he was so sexy and funny, that I just went with the flow. But now with him pulling up to this restaurant, I was a little bit curious.

"I'm a sports agent to a lot of NBA players," he mentioned casually. He acted like he told me that he was working in an office. I was very impressed. He carried himself in such a way you would never think he had a cool job like that.

"That's nice." I nodded.

"It's okay." He shrugged it off. "Come on."

He led me to the restaurant. The hostess was there and she greeted us. I was so used to hostess being warm and friendly, but she just seemed out of it.

"What's going on?" he asked her.

"Nothing, just had this bad experience with this customer. She came in with her boyfriend or whatever and had this attitude. Before she even let me speak, she cut me off demanding that she got a great table." She rolled her eyes.

"I'm sorry to hear that. I hope that she left

a nice tip at least." I suggested and she shook her head.

"I don't want nothing to do with her." She smiled. "I just blame myself because someone cancelled their reservation which is why I let them in, but it's whatever. Do you guys have a reservation though?" Kamel told her his name and she went through a list. "Yes, there you are. May you please follow me?"

We followed her through this gorgeous restaurant to this private section. There were other people here but it was pretty secluded. When we got to our booth, I noticed that it was candlelit and looked super romantic.

"Ok, you guys are here and your waiter will be with you any moment." The hostess told us. We thanked her and Kamel immediately pulled the chair out for me.

"Such a gentleman," I cooed.

"I try."

The whole date was going great. I didn't know why I was so nervous. It was probably because of everything I went through with both Darius and Shane. I just didn't want to jump in too quick, but like Dr. Wood suggested… this was just a date. I wasn't running off to marry him and I was not even calling him my boyfriend just yet, but it was still nice to be spending time with someone.

"I wonder what I should eat," I thought out loud, looking over the menu.

"Well don't worry, you can have whatever you want." He smiled. "Let's see if they have a kid menu though," he joked.

"You cheap—"

"Uh uh." He laughed while interrupting me. "You can ball out on the kids' menu." He looked down at the menu. "There is no kids' section though." He winked at me. "Oh, darn." He playfully shrugged his shoulders. "I'll guess I'll clip some coupons…" he went on and I kept laughing. His face was so silly so he couldn't be serious. Besides, this man was a sports agent and was dropping luxury cars; I thought he could afford dinner with no problem.

We kept laughing and it felt like we'd been there for few minutes, but it was really a long time. I could have had so much more fun with Kamel, but then I felt someone staring at me. You know that intense feeling of heat? The type of heat you can only feel when you know that someone is looking at you. I was talking to Kamel, but I was also looking around to see who was looking at me. I finally caught their eyes and I dropped my fork on my plate.

"Is everything okay?" Kamel asked and I just babbled on and on about me having butterfingers. I tried to make him feel like everything is okay. What was I supposed to do? Was I supposed to tell him that I just spotted my ex, Shane, in the restaurant?

When Kamel wasn't paying attention, I looked back to where I saw Shane. I just had to make sure it was him and not me making things up. Looking back at the table, I saw that he was looking back at me. It was him alright, but not only that...he was with an attractive woman! I only saw the side of her face, but I knew she had to be beautiful to be with Shane. I hated the feeling of jealousy that popped up. How could I feel this way when I was here with Kamel? It didn't help that Shane was still looking good either. Even from this distance, I could still see how sexy he was. Damn.

We were staring at each other and in those moments, it was like our eyes were having a conversation. There was so much that could be said with just our eyes. He kept looking at me, but then he looked at Kamel. I wasn't sure if I saw sadness in his eyes, but I know that it looked like he understood. When he started to look at me like he used to in the past, I had to turn my head. Just that one stare down was bringing back feelings that I thought were gone.

"So, shall we have some desert?" I suggested, trying to focus back on my date.

We ordered this chocolate lava cake. We both were so excited because it turned out we both had a huge love of chocolate and all things sweet. I couldn't wait and even though Shane was some feet away, I knew that this chocolate would make me forgot about him...if only for a little while.

Suddenly we heard some footsteps coming our way and I just knew that was the waiter coming with the desert. I turned and saw this woman walking in. She definitely wasn't part of the staff because she had on sweats and her hair was in a ponytail. She gave me a quick look of attitude, but when she looked at Kamel, I saw straight fire and hate coming through her eyes.

"What the hell you think you're doing, Kamel?" She asked him, standing right next to our table with her arms crossed.

I sat there, not knowing what to do. How did this woman know his name? I tried to find some clues to what was going on with him, but he looked just as confused as me.

"I'm sorry?" he asked sounding so puzzled. "What do you mean?"

"Don't do that shit Kamel!" she warned him with her finger in her face. "You got me all the way fucked up if you think you're going to play stupid."

"I don't know what you're talking about." He sounded so lost and I was too. Just what was going on?

"Kamel, who is she?" I asked.

"His wife, bitch, do you have a problem?"

"Wife?" I repeated and started to push myself away from the table.

"Yup!" She nodded and looked right back at Kamel. "His *wife*."

To say I was embarrassed wasn't enough. I was embarrassed, of course, but even more than that, I was pissed off.

"Look, I didn't know," I started. "I'm sorry about all of this."

"Mhmm," she replied.

"You can have him. I don't do married men." I looked back at Kamel. His face said it all. He had been caught in his lie. "Dirty dog!" I grabbed the glass of wine and threw it in his face. I slammed the glass on the table and walked right out of the restaurant.

CHAPTER 8

Jayla

I started pacing in front of the restaurant. I was trying to cool down, but I was still in shock and disbelief over what just happened. Kamel was married? I tried to think back to his hands and if I ever saw a wedding ring on them. I couldn't picture it and I knew that was one of the first things I always looked for. Married men who cheat are such pieces of shit. They will create a whole new life just to get some on the side. Shaking my head, I was reminded of the days of Darius. How is this happening to me again? At least the blessing was that I didn't get too invested with Kamel. But damn, Kamel was not only married but he was my ride out here. Now I have to take an Uber home. Fucking ridiculous.

"The hostess told me to give this to you." His voice brought back memories and I closed my eyes before looking at him. I had to brace myself but when I looked at him, I still wasn't ready. He was the last person I wanted to see after everything that went down. Damn, why did that have to happen with Shane there to watch it all? I looked in his hand and saw that he had a box. I opened it up and it was a small chocolate cake. I guess the hostess saw what happened and gave me the dessert instead.

"Thank you," I said softly.

"How are you doing?"

"Oh, I'm just fine." I smiled widely. "Just peachy. The guy I just started to see was married so you know, it's nothing but good news over here."

"I'm sorry that happened." He was trying to comfort me.

"Me too."

"How are you getting home?" He saw me looking at my phone.

"Uber, but all the rides are far so it's going to be a wait."

"Don't worry about that, I'll take you home."

I don't know why, but I laughed so hard that I snorted.

"You take me home?" I shook my head. "With who? Your date?" I snapped. "I think not."

"My date is nothing to worry about. She was boring and not my type."

"Hmm, I'm sure." I rolled my eyes.

"Look, if my date was important, what am I doing out here with you? Why am I checking up on you?" he asked. "She's nothing and she's still there probably trying to figure out where it all went wrong." He went on but I wasn't buying it. "I still care about you, Jayla."

Those last six words made me spin my head around. I looked into his eyes and could see how genuine he is. Next thing I knew I was strolling along memory lane. All the good times that we shared together, flashed before my head. It was me and him and all the love that we had. This man, after everything we went through, honestly still cared for me. Even though he hasn't seen me or heard from me in months, he still cared.

"May I please take you home? I don't want you have to stand out here any longer than you have to. You've been through enough."

"Okay." I gave in. "You can take me home."

We started walking to his car and it felt awkward. I wanted to say something, but my tongue was tied. Out of nowhere, I felt his jacket around my shoulders.

"It's kind of chilly out here." He made sure that it was on. "You're good?"

"I'm fine, thank you." I smiled at him because I needed him to know that it was okay. It felt tense between us and I wanted him to know that there wasn't any beef between us. He gave me a small smirk and then chirped his car. He opened my door and let me in. He got in the driver's seat and sighed.

We didn't speak and he didn't start the car right away. It was kind of weird, but tonight was a weird night.

"You ready?" he asked after he finally

started the car. I nodded and we were off. He had the radio on and he played some smooth R&B. The mixture of his scent, the music, and the memories that ran through my head was all too much. All these things coming together just made me miss him so much. I glanced at him slightly and almost wanted to reach out and touch him. Even though we'd been through a lot, I still wanted to be with him. I'd been holding back these feelings for so long, that now that they were here…. I felt them all ten times strong.

We got to my house and he got out and opened the door. I paused standing next to him and had to stop myself from kissing his lips. It felt strange not to do it. I was so used to us kissing after a date, but then I had to remind myself that I just came from a disastrous date with Kamel. Even Shane had a bad date with that chick on the same night. What were the chances? I finally moved and stood next to the door. I started fumbling in my purse looking for my keys. I only had about two other items, but I was taking my time. I felt the words that I really wanted to say stuck in my throat. They were dying to coming out, but I wasn't brave enough to say them. I had to settle for something else.

"Would you like to come in?"

His eyes opened wide. He wasn't expecting that but he smiled as soon as I offered.

"Are you sure?"

"It's been a weird night for the both of us. How about you come in and we have like a small nightcap?" His smile grew wider and he put the alarm on his car. I opened up my door wide and he walked in. I closed the door behind him and took a deep breath in.

Seeing him in my house made me feel different. It was strange in a way, but still it felt right. He looked around and could see that not much has changed. His eyes went to Keon's room.

"Oh, Keon is with his girlfriend Crystal. She just got a new apartment so they are almost there all the time."

"That's nice." He turned around and looked at me. "But I know you miss them."

"Listen, I want the best for my brother," I told him. "But I do miss him being around," I confessed and we both laughed.

"So, we're alone," he stated.

"Yup….just me and you."

Slowly, I made my way over to the kitchen. I reached and got out a new bottle of Moscato.

"I know you're not crazy about these drinks, but would you like a glass?" I called out over my shoulder.

"Sure." Hearing his voice so close to me made me jump. "I'm sorry," he apologized. "I didn't mean to scare you."

"It's not that," I reassured him. "I just thought you were sitting on the couch."

"I thought that I should help you." He was looking directly into my eyes. He walked over to me and stood right next to me. His tall body was towering over me and his scent was every-where. I felt a part of my body jump for him, but I held back. He reached over me and went into the cabinets to get two wine glasses.

Later, we sat on the couch and he told me a little bit of his awful date.

"Wow it sounds like she had some big plans for you." I laughed.

"She did, but it completely turned me off. Every time that she spoke it just told me that I wasn't interested in her; maybe I never was."

"That's sad."

"It's not." He looked me in the eyes. "That bad date led me to be here with you."

"Is that a good thing?" I asked, not looking at him. I was tracing my finger around my wine glass.

"Of course it is Jayla. I can't tell you how much I've missed you."

"You have?"

"Every single day."

"I've missed you too."

With those words finally out, I felt this burden lift from me. I finally let go of that secret and it was such a relief.

"Jayla, I know I've said this a million times, but I am sorry for all that has happened to you. I never meant for you to be in danger in any way."

"I know that," I replied. "I've thought about it a lot over these past months. I've even been in counseling."

"I'm sorry."

"No, that's a good thing. I really needed to talk to someone else about this. I had a lot to get out and I've worked through a lot of things."

"I'm glad to hear that."

We started drinking a little bit more and he told me about his plans for his gyms. He really was taking it to a whole other level. The thought of a massage after a workout was so smart. It made sense. You could take a quick shower and then go to a spa. He was trying to make sure that people not only took care of their physical health, but also their mental. I had to applaud him for his business mind. He always thought a step ahead.

"Enough about work." He put his wine glass down and took my hand softly. "I can't keep talking about that when all I want to do is talk about us."

"Us?"

"Yes, us. I miss you and I miss us." He kissed the back of my hand.

"I miss it too." I slid closer to him on the couch. "I wish none of that shit happened."

"Me too." He looked a little sad in his eyes and I knew he was thinking of all the drama that I went through. To see him get a little emotional about what I'd been through made me have all types of feels. The next thing I knew, I was leaning in and kissing his lips.

The second our lips touched, our clothes started flying off. I just needed to touch him again. I needed to be with him again. And by the way he was grabbing me, and kissing me, he needed it as much as I did. When we both got down to our underwear, I jumped in his arms and he brought me to my bedroom. He laid me on top of my sheets and kissed me all over. Between each kiss he kept telling me how much he missed me.

"I've been thinking about you for so long." He kissed my neck and bit it softly. "I've missed you. I've missed touching you." He bit into my shoulder and grabbed my ass. I moaned out loud and felt myself get more excited. His hand slid between my legs and chuckled when he felt how turned on I was. "I've missed that too." Within seconds, he had my legs opened and he started to taste me.

These past few months, I'd often thought about his tongue, but I'd forgotten how good his tongue was. His tongue was in each and every part of me. It danced in and out of holes, folds, and flaps. I kept howling because every time my legs shook, I leaked out.

"It's so good!" I called out. His eyes locked

with mine and he started going even crazier. My body was moving wildly and I had no control of it anymore. The intense heat took over my whole body and I released everything. I started breathing hard and when he came back up, he had this slick look on his face.

"Game on."

I put him on the bed, climbed on top of him, and slowly slid down. Whirling my hips around, I was about to get him back. It took me a minute to get my speed up because he wore me out, but when I saw that he had his eyes closed, that fed my ego and I continued to please him. I put his hands on my ass and I started to bounce up and down, just the way he liked it. He started to help me along and our bodies clapped together in rhythm. It sounded like we were getting a round of applause for all our efforts. He grunted to let me know that he was almost there, so I slowed down. I wanted to cherish this moment. He got the cue and flipped himself so that he could be on top.

Looking into his eyes, I kept leaning up to kiss him. I'd really missed those lips and him. He went slowly and as he looked at me, I felt all the love that he was giving me. Not just physically, but there was such a connection, that I couldn't deny that a part of me was falling in love all over again. I wanted to say the words to him, but it felt like it was too soon. So for now, I was just going to enjoy the amazing sex.

Shane and I went round after round and after round of sex. Every time we finished, all we had to do was just look at each other and we started all over again. Finally after some hours, we laid there in each other's arms. This felt so right and this is how it always should have been. I should be with Shane. I knew he was the man for me. When Dr. Wood suggested that I take some time to heal, he was right. He knew that if I went back to Shane before now, I would not have been ready. I was really angry back then and a lot of what had happened wasn't Shane's fault at all. Even though I was in a lot of drama, right now, in his arms, I felt so safe. I knew this was where I belonged.

Shane was starting to fall asleep and I just kept staring at him. I refuse to let this be a one-night thing. I needed for him to be back in my life, and I knew what I had to do. I had to truly forgive Shane for all that had happened. It wasn't his fault that Damiah went crazy. He did do all that he could to stop it and he saved my life. If Shane didn't have a gut feeling that something was going wrong that day, I could have been dead.

"I forgive you," I whispered, and he didn't move, but I felt better saying those words. I needed to say it out loud. He didn't hear me and that was okay. I wasn't saying it for Shane; it was for me. I gave him a soft peck on his lips and began to fall asleep.

The following morning, I woke up slowly. Memories of last night was running through my head. I was smiling and felt really happy. I turned to feel for Shane, but he wasn't there. I grabbed a shirt, put it on, and found him in the kitchen making breakfast.

"Oooh, what is this?" I asked as I watched him chop up green peppers. He threw it in the pan with the scrambled eggs. "It smells nice in here." I looked at all the groceries spread out in the kitchen. "Did you go grocery shopping?" I asked and he nodded his head, but then shook it no.

"Not really. I used this app so someone else would do the grocery shopping for me. I got you some fresh fruit and freshly squeezed orange juice."

"You're spoiling me." My eyes opened wide at the croissants. "Ugh, I love these!" I grabbed one and breathed it in deeply. "Let me brush my teeth real quick and I'll join you."

When I finished getting ready, I saw that Shane had the table set. There was croissants, eggs, juices, and fresh fruit.

"Damn, you got it looking like a little restaurant in here. I should take a pic of this for the 'Gram," I joked.

"You're too funny," he said in a plain voice. "Come on, let's eat."

Three bites or so into the meal and Shane cleared his throat.

"I really don't want to kill the vibe, but I got to bring it up."

"Last night?" I questioned.

"Yeah." He put his fork down and looked at me. "About last night…"

"I just really missed you."

"I missed you too, but I can't and won't pretend that it was just about sex."

"I know it's not."

"I want you back in my life and not on some sex shit. I want you back as my girl."

My smile grew across my face quickly. I was going to play it off, but I didn't care if he saw how happy that statement made me.

"I want to be back too, but we're going to have to have some rules. I need you to be 100% honest with me. I understood why you hid Damiah, I get it, but I can't have anything like that happening again. Just tell me the truth."

"I promise. And I need something from you."

"Me?"

"Yes. if I do something wrong, which I'm never plan on doing, I need you to hear me out. I'm not going to lie, it hurt that you just closed me off. I get why you did it, but it still hurt."

"I had to do it for me."

"I get that Jayla, I'm not faulting you for that, but the next time, please just hear me out. Don't go completely cold on me."

"I promise." I grabbed the cup of orange juice and held it out. "New beginnings?"

"New beginnings." We cheered each other and smiled. "You're so goofy," he teased.

"Ah, you hater." I stuck my tongue out.

Later that day, we got to watching some Netflix. Samara called and asked if she could take his son to the park and it was perfect. We just had the whole day to ourselves. With Keon still at Crystal's place, we sat on the couch and just watched comedies and musicals. Shane made fun of my horrible singing, but I didn't care. I was going to try to hit the notes like 1990's Mariah Carey. When that was finally over, we watched some romantic comedies. I swear we barely moved off of the couch. He ordered Chinese and we just stayed there in our own little bubble. It was so peaceful. It felt like the whole bullshit with Damiah never went down. It felt like that simple loving relationship I'd been looking for. It was so perfect and I hoped this happiness would last this time.

CHAPTER 9

Jayla

My relationship with Shane almost seemed to change overnight. Since the date that we decided to wipe the slate clean, we'd been around each other all the time. It had been five months and each day I found something new to love about Shane. I thought I really loved Shane before, but the man that I was with now, I was head over heels in love with. Not only was he a great man to me, but he was an excellent father to his son. A few weeks ago, I met his son and I was nervous. I guessed because so much about him was tied up with Damiah, but when that little boy came up to me and hugged me, I just wanted to keep him. He was so adorable and polite that it was hard not to fall for him too.

I loved going over to Shane's house because his son always greeted me with a picture. He would draw these stick figures and have a background story with them. It wasn't that long before he started drawing me into his pictures. In one of them, he made me taller than his Dad and Shane was confused.

"Why?" he asked his son and all that little man replied was that he wanted to make me taller, so that was it. I laughed and gave him a hug.

Today was a long day at work. Sadly one of the patients had to be transferred to the hospital. I hated when that happened. I'd always grown attached to the patients, so when they left, it felt like family left too. I came home and just wanted to soak in the tub. By the time I got to my front door, I saw that there were some lights on. I knew that Keon, of course, was spending some time at his girl-friend's house. I walked in slowly and my mouth dropped. There were electric candles everywhere and two huge bouquet of roses on the table. Next to this display, there was this envelope. I opened it and saw a card that had a teddy bear holding a heart. Shane was always being sweet to me. I opened the card and two pieces of paper fell out. The card read, "Take some time off work. We need to relax." I picked up the papers and saw that it was two tickets to the Bahamas.

I started screaming. I couldn't believe it. In my hand, I held two first class tickets to the Bahamas.

"What the hell?" Keon came in. "Are you okay? I can hear you screaming from like a block away. I thought some shit was going down." He put his backpack down on the couch. "What's all this shit?" He looked at all the candles and roses. I still could barely speak so I handed him the tickets and the card. He read it and then smiled. "Damn Sis, that's a good look. Shit, can I come too?"

We both busted out laughing.

"Boy I'm not going to take you on my baecation with Shane."

"Damn Sis, ya won't even see me. I'll be at the other end of the resort or whatever. I'll bring Crystal and we'll just chill."

"Nuh uh. I love ya, but this is for me and Shane."

"Fine, if that's how you want it," he joked. "But seriously though, you should go. You've earned it. Not only because you work hard, look after me and Crystal, but because you been through a lot and you need a change of scenery."

"You think so?"

"If you don't use these tickets, just know that me and Crystal will be sippin something good instead of you. Go enjoy and have a vacation, baecation, whatever you just called it."

"You're right." I looked at the tickets once more. "How can I turn it down? I'm not saying 'no' to this."

Three weeks later I was in the Bahamas with Shane. We had our own private villa that came with our own private beach. The first few days we spent most of it having sex and making love everywhere. Shane would just look at me a certain way and the next thing I knew, I was bent over. It was nice. And when we weren't having sex, we were just enjoying each other's company. We ate at some of the local restaurants, had a couples' massage, and took a day trip.

Today the sun was rising and as always it was beautiful. I got out my phone and took a picture of me standing in front of the sunrise. When I looked at my selfie, I noticed how happy and at peace I looked. Not only because of this great vacation, but it was beyond amazing to wake up with Shane every morning. There was this look of happiness he had when we got up in the morning together. It was the same look that I saw in the selfie right now.

Later that day, I took a vid of all the things that we did. I was enjoying my week long baecation. On the last day, we took a nice romantic walk on the beach. We took a picture together and I looked at how happy we were.

"I'm so glad we came out here," I told him the last night we were there. "Thank you for bringing us out here."

"Thank you for taking the time to come out. I know that couldn't have been easy, but I'm glad you did."

"Keon said that if I didn't come, he was going to take our tickets."

"Keon and I had our little thing in the past, but that's my boy right now. With that being said, there was no was I was going to let him use these tickets."

That night, I came out to beach wearing practically nothing. He was on this phone finalizing the details to the gym's expansion when I got on top of him. He was taken by surprise, but naturally we started kissing. He went to kissing my neck and I felt him rise against me. He didn't even try to take off what little I had on; he just moved it to the side and slid inside of me. I bit my lip as we both moved together in the same rhythm. It didn't take long for us both to explode.

"I'm going to miss this place," I whispered in his ear as I laid on top of him. We listened to the sound of the water crashing against the sand.

"Me too." He held onto me tightly as our vacation was coming to an end.

CHAPTER 10

Jayla

We came back to the States refreshed and rested. It was exactly what we needed. That baecation brought us closer together, but we had to come back. I had to continue working at the nursing home and Shane's new gym was going to open in just a week. He was running around like crazy making sure that everything was fine, but his friend Tone kept telling him to relax. The day of the opening, Shane wanted everything to be special, so he told me to invite anyone who I wanted there. Naturally, I wanted Keon and Crystal there;

that was a given. I tried to get my little sister to come visit, but it was the week of her midterms and we both agreed that her studies came first. So instead I brought down my girls Kim and Charmaine.

They got off the plane and I was there to pick them up at the airport.

"Look at these two bishes!" I screamed as I ran towards them. We hugged and kissed. Kim looked so good and Charmaine was glowing.

"Girrrrrrrrrrrrl," Charmaine said in only the way she could. "I felt like I haven't seen you in like a million years."

"What are you talking about? We're on Skype all the time."

"You know that's not the same," Kim butted in. "But, I'm glad we're here."

"Yeah, me too. Shane wanted me to have some familiar faces at his grand opening. He told me it was to thank me for all that I've done for the gym. I've helped him pick out some colors and even with the people he hired."

"Well damn girl, you might as well be the manager of the place." Kim laughed.

"I'll do anything for that man," I told them.

"Someone is in love." Charmaine smiled.

"Deeply." I giggled.

It was the time of the opening and it seemed like all of Houston was there. Shane had purchased so many ads and it paid off. The new gym was packed and that said a lot considering it was a three-floor building. There was a lot of press too and everyone was talking about how this gym changed the game. With the healthy food and now masseuses and chiropractors, there was nothing like it. I even convinced him to get some people that specialized in acupuncture. He was a little skeptical, but he eventually did that too. Now with all these new services, the gym seemed unstoppable.

"Ladies and gentlemen, I want to thank you all for coming out." Shane started with his speech. He reached for my hand and had me standing close to him. "Everyone here has worked so hard to make this gym happen. I know it was a bold move to add the services that I did, but I just thought we should change how we look at gyms. It simply can't be a place where you out; there has to be more. So, within the next few hours, we will open our services and everyone here gets 50% off on membership and the add on services." People started to applaud and I was smiling like crazy. I was so proud of Shane.

"It means a lot to me to have you all here and especially this young lady." He looked at me and kissed the back of my hand. "I honestly, don't know what I'd do without her. She made sure that I didn't go too crazy and she gave input and honest feedback. She's such a rare gem, that I don't think she knows how much I appreciate her. We've had our rocky road, but that didn't stop us. She's loving, giving, honest, and one of the biggest blessings I've had in my life thus far. I never thought I could love a woman as much as I love her."

People started snapping pictures of us and I smiled for all of them. Shane was always finding a way to make me feel appreciated and I loved that.

"That's why—" He handed his drink to Keon to hold and then he dropped down to one knee. Once I saw him down there, I started crying immediately. Charmaine and Kim broke out in cheers and screams first. Samara gasped and covered her mouth. Everyone started clapping and cheering while I was crying.

"That's why I have to make it official," he told them but was looking at me. "I know our love story wasn't perfect, but I wouldn't trade it for anything because look at where it got us. I fall in love with you every day Jayla, and I want to continue to do that for the rest of my life." I was nodding and crying and then he reached into his pocket and pulled out a ring box. He opened it slowly and I saw this huge rock. "Would you do me the honor of being my wife?"

Everyone started cheering. Keon looked so happy and Crystal was in tears. I kept trying to speak but I was so moved that it got harder to do so. I just couldn't help but to think of the road that brought us here. All the bullshit with Damiah, the fact that I almost died, and me wanting nothing but a normal relationship. I kept begging for something simple after all the drama, but I was given something extraordinary instead. I looked into his eyes and I knew that this man was going to fight for me and our love for the rest of our lives. There was clearly only one answer to give. I nodded and then said "yes" which caused everyone to cheer and applause like crazy. He slid the ring on my finger, and then got up to kiss me.

Kim, Charmaine, and Crystal all ran up to me. We started hugging and screaming in happiness. Was this really my life? Throughout the party, people kept coming up to me congratulating me, but it didn't feel real. Across the room, I watched Tone, Keon, and Shane all talking to each other. Keon shook his hand and patted him on his back. Shane smiled and then he turned to look at me. I gave him a wide smile and blew him a kiss. Yes, this was my life and everything was falling into the place.

"How do you feel?" Samara asked me. I took a deep breath and thought of everything.

"I'm so happy," I said holding back tears.

Despite all the drama, I finally had my

happy ending. And after all the shit that I went through, I deserved every moment.

❧

To FIND *out when Mia Black has new books available, follow* Mia Black on Instagram: @authormiablack